Snip, Snip ... SNOW!

Nancy Poydar

Holiday House/New York

For Doris Louise with love

Copyright © 1997 by Nancy Poydar
All rights reserved
Printed in the United States of America

Library of Congress Cataloging-in-Publication Data
Poydar, Nancy.
Snip, Snip . . . SNOW! / Nancy Poydar, [author and illustrator].
p.   cm.
Summary: Sophie wants it to snow and anxiously awaits a predicted
snowstorm. Includes instructions for making paper snowflakes.
ISBN 0-8234-1328-4
[1. Snow—Fiction.]   I. Title.
PZ7.P8846So   1997   97-9052   CIP   AC
[E]—dc21
ISBN 0-8234-1415-9 (pbk.)

Sophie thought it would never snow.
The trees were bare.
The ground was hard.
The air was crisp.
But there was no snow.

When Sophie went outside,
she had to wear her heavy jacket,
mittens, and her hood,
but there was no snow.
Noses were chilly.
Cheeks were rosy.
You could see your own breath!
But there was no snow.

"No snow!" Sophie said,
 as she stomped into the house after school.
"It's nice without snow," said Sophie's mom.
"No snowballs," said Sophie.
"No snow on the walk," Mom said.
"No snow on the sledding hill," Sophie complained.
"No shoveling," Mom added.
"No snowman," Sophie grumbled.

One evening
the weatherman
forecast snow.
"Snow,"
sighed Mom.
"Snow!"
squealed Sophie.

"Snow.

Snow.

SNOW!"

"I'm afraid snow's
  in the forecast,"
  announced Sophie's dad.
"We know,"
  said Mom.
"We know!"
  said Sophie.

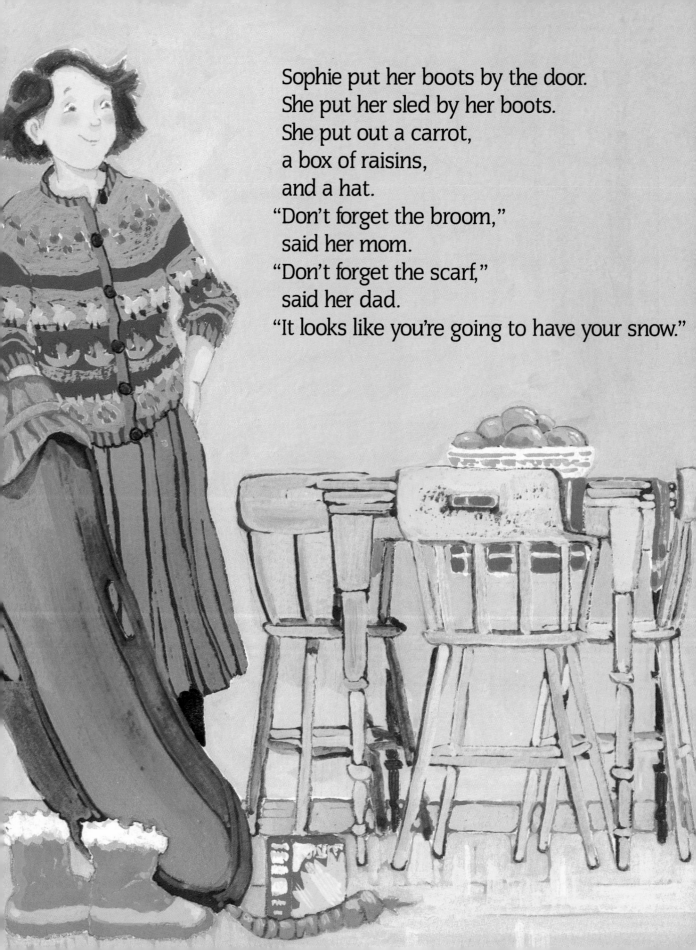

Sophie put her boots by the door.
She put her sled by her boots.
She put out a carrot,
a box of raisins,
and a hat.
"Don't forget the broom,"
said her mom.
"Don't forget the scarf,"
said her dad.
"It looks like you're going to have your snow."

Sophie could hardly eat.

But she did.

Sophie could hardly sleep.

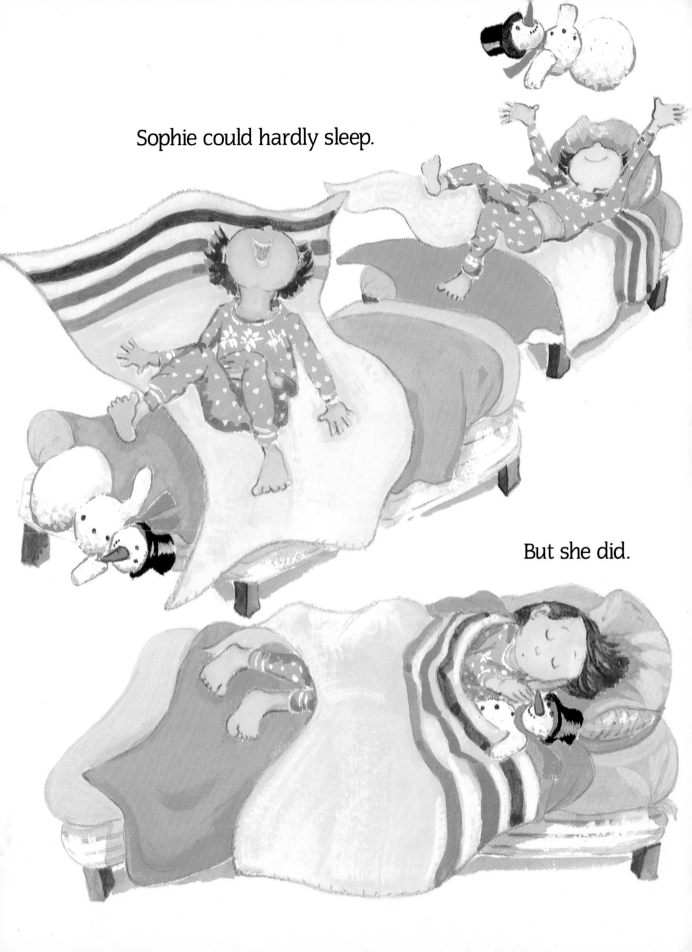

But she did.

In the morning, though,
when she looked outside,
the ground was still bare!
"Where's my snow?"
"Your storm is stalled," said her dad.
"We might not get it at all."

Sophie thought
her mom and dad
looked too pleased.

At school, Sophie asked
if they could make their own snow.
"Please. Please. Please!" she begged.
Mrs. Bloom let Sophie give everyone
a stack of white paper and scissors.

They folded and snipped and folded and snipped.
Each snowflake was a surprise.
No two were alike in the whole classroom.
Sophie made an extra snowflake to take home later.

"Look at our floor," sighed Mrs. Bloom.
"We made it snow in here!" cried Sophie.
"Time to clean up," Mrs. Bloom said brightly.
"Time to plow and shovel," Sophie mumbled.

Sophie made a paper snowman out of the scraps by her chair.
"I'm recycling," she told Mrs. Bloom.
  Sophie taped her snowman to the window.
"Oh," she said as she peered outside . . .

Teeny, tiny flakes were wafting through the gray sky.
Teeny, tiny flakes were falling through the bare branches.
They softly settled on the swings and the slide.
They softly settled on the school steps and on the window sill
"Shhh," said Mrs. Bloom, and she opened the window a little.
"Hear how quietly they fall."

On the way home, the snow came faster.
Sophie caught the flakes on her mitten.
No two were alike.
They were beautiful.

"Snow!" she yelled to her mom.
"I know," her mom said.
"It's beautiful."
"Shhh," whispered Sophie,
and she held the door open.
"Hear how quietly they fall."
"There's going to be
plenty of snow," said her mom.
"Enough for snowballs?" asked Sophie.
"Enough for your boots," said Mom.
"Enough for sledding?" squealed Sophie.
"Enough for your snowman," Mom said.

And the next morning, there was!

SOPHIE'S SNOWFLAKE

You will need white paper and scissors.

1. Draw a circle on the paper and cut it out. You may trace around a dinner plate or something else that is round.

2. Fold the circle in half.

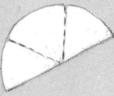

3. Fold the half into thirds.

4. Fold this shape down the middle.

5. Now snip little pieces out of the three sides.

6. Unfold and enjoy your snowflake! No two will be alike.